CORNFLAKE GIRL

TORI AMOS

PHOTOGRAPHIC CREDITS

FRONT COVER: Derek Ridgers © LONDON FEATURES INTERNATIONAL

BACK COVER: Niels Van Iperen © RETNA

© ALL ACTION

© REDFERNS

© RETNA

For more information write to;
UFO Music 18 Hanway Street London W1P 9DD England
Telephone: 0171 636 1281   Fax: 0171 636 0738

First published in Great Britain 1996
UFO Music Ltd 18 Hanway Street
London W1P 9DD

The author and publishers have made every effort to contact all copyright
holders. Any who for any reason have not been contacted are invited to write to
the publishers so that a full acknowledgment may be made in subsequent
editions of this work.

ISBN 1-873884-56-7

Designed by UFO Music Ltd

Printed by Butler & Tanner

TORI AMOS

CORNFLAKE GIRL   SUSAN WILSON

1
EVERYBODY ELSE'S GIRL

On August 22nd, 1963, Mary Ellen Amos, wife to Dr Edison Amos, gave birth to her third child, a girl, at the Old Catawba Hospital in Newton, North Carolina. Later, when the child was a woman, she would proclaim that this life was the latest in a long line of existences, including that of a Viking, and that it was she who had chosen to join this new family.

If the choice to enter the Amos line was indeed hers, it turned out to be a painful, although insightful one. The strict Methodist upbringing it dealt out stifled her sexuality during adolescence, but later drove her into discovering a unique language of her own. And the Cherokee blood coursing through her veins from her mother's side gave her a vital spiritual connection with life beyond that sought out by organised religion. Tightly bound in one sense and roaming free in another, the child was placed in a backdrop of contradiction which would ultimately spur her on to spin a sea of creativity.

The baby was given a name - Myra Ellen Amos, and grew up on a mixed diet of earth mythology, dream spells and natural medicine from her mother's parents, stirred up by the grim morality lessons dealt out by her father's. Bertie Marie Akins Copeland was her Cherokee-descended Nannie, Calvin Clinton Copeland, her beloved Poppa, who sang to her and told her Cherokee tales from the day she was born. In stark contrast were her parental grandmother, also secretly labelled her Victorian grandmother, Addie Allen Amos, and her grandfather James W. Amos, both of whom were ordained ministers and missionaries.

"My grandmother on my father's side believed all girls should be virgins," Tori told Liz Evans in her book, *Women, Sex And Rock'n'Roll* in 1994, "And if you didn't come that way to your husband you were not one of God's children and you'd go to hell."

Myra Ellen was 13 when Addie Allen died, but the damage was done. Shame had been instilled into her, and although she managed to defy the judgmental voices which were left ringing in her ears to some extent, it was never without feeling unbearably guilty.

"When I was little I got into big trouble for wondering if Jesus had a thing going with Mary Magdelene." Tori later told Andy Darling in the November 28th, 1991 edition of *The Guardian*.

"I had a really big crush on Jesus." she confided to Steve Malins in the May 1994 edition

of *VOX*, **"I used to think that I would be a really good girlfriend for him."**

Long before Myra Ellen was to encounter sex and all its confusion however, she was developing a rare musical talent. Her elder brother and sister used to practice on the family piano at home in Baltimore, Maryland, and at the age of two and a half, she was bashing out little tunes to herself before she could speak. By the time she was five, she'd discovered The Beatles *Sgt Pepper's Lonely Hearts Club Band* album lying around the house, and declared that this was what she was going to do, but her parents had already realised the potential of their gifted child, and in the hope of training her up to concert pianist level, they took her to audition at Baltimore's prestigious Peabody Conservatory Of Music. Despite being uncomfortably aware of herself having to perform as if she were some kind of curio, Myra Ellen won a scholarship, making her the youngest student ever to be accepted by the institute.

For the next six years, Myra Ellen spent her weeks at regular school, and her Saturdays at the Peabody. She enjoyed her weekend world of music, but as the months and years went by, she began to feel increasingly frustrated by the disciplinarian methods employed by the institute. They put money on her wrists in an effort to make her play 'correctly', they didn't appreciate her spontaneously inventing original tunes, and they found her unorthodox character a little alarming. During the week, at normal school, it was a similar story. Separated from the rest of the class for chatting to her neighbours and causing what were deemed to be disturbances, Myra Ellen was treated like an academic slowhand because of her one outstanding musical talent.

Sundays were of course taken up with church, confusing her life even further. Myra Ellen's only refuge was found during the summertime, which she spent with her Nannie and Poppa in North Carolina.

But when she was nine, Myra Ellen's Poppa died. She was devastated.

"I would go to his grave all the time." she told Mat Snow in the February 1994 edition of Q magazine.

Her mother believes Myra Ellen never really got over Poppa's death. For four years she sang to him at his graveside.

By this time, the Amos family had relocated to Silver Spring, Maryland. Myra Ellen was no longer a sweet little thing, and suddenly found herself being singled out for criticism by the older women of the new church her father was assigned to. Upset and confused, she continued to attend the Peabody, as well as private tuition sessions, and began to discover the likes of Jimi Hendrix, Led Zeppelin and The Doors through the older Peabody students. She developed a huge crush on Led Zeppelin's singer, Robert Plant, and harboured a desire to lose her

virginity to him. Growing up in such a strict environment at home hadn't suppressed her primal instincts, but when she was ten her first period started in a school playground and she was completely unprepared.

"My mother hadn't told me anything about it," she told Steve Malins in the May 1994 edition of *VOX* magazine, **"I thought I was going to die."**

By now Myra Ellen had had her first joint and was merrily flicking through copies of Playgirl magazine with her friends. To not know about periods at her stage in life was absurd as well as frightening.

Eventually, at the age of 11, Myra Ellen was effectively thrown out of the Peabody. Her scholarship was not renewed, and as the family had no money, the option for her to stay on was simply not there. Myra Ellen felt relieved. She had had enough of the discipline, and she knew that all she really wanted was to compose, which the Peabody had discouraged her from doing. But she was also left with the overwhelming sense of having failed her father, a feeling which was to haunt her for many years to come. All hopes for her to graduate with a doctorate at the age of 18 had vanished. The respectable concert pianist career had skipped off the horizon.

As a consequence of letting down her family, Myra Ellen fell into a depression which kept her well away from the piano. Mike, her elder brother and main musical collaborator had left home to marry and her sister departed for college. Alone at home with her parents, without the musical weekends at the Peabody, Myra Ellen's spirits plummeted. Dr Amos encouraged her to re-audition for the Peabody, but her wilful rendition of *'I've Been Cheated'* did not impress the board of examiners, and she was refused readmission.

Now free to explore her *'rock star'* leanings, she continued to sing and play in church and in school musicals, and won the county Teen Talent Contest in 1977. Her parents quickly realised that their daughter was not about to give up on music, even though she was no longer on the safe and steady path she had been. They understood that it was in all their best interests to encourage her, despite their obvious disappointment at her fate. So Dr Amos decided, almost ironically considering his religious views, to help her continue her musical career in Baltimore's gay bars.

"I think he came to realise that you either supported your kid or you lost them," said Tori in *Women, Sex And Rock'n'Roll*, **"And a lot of my friends were getting pregnant. A lot of them had had abortions by the time they were 14."**

Tori's father also understood the importance of fulfiling one's own true ambitions. He had been pressurised into the ministry by his parents, and would probably have been **"James Dean or a doctor"** according to his daughter. He spent his whole life trying to please his parents, who repaid him by criticising his sermons.

Myra Ellen was just 13 when her father began to chaperone her during her evening performances at Mr Henry's and Mr Smith's where he attracted more male attention than she did with his dashing looks and dog collar. Wearing her sister's polyester pants and generous helpings of make up, she managed to look older than her years, and has very fond memories of the audiences and the club staff she encountered at the time. Plied with non-alcoholic daquiris, she was taught how to give blow jobs with a cucumber by the waiters - the test was to leave no teeth marks.

Over the next few years Myra Ellen played in musicals, tried her hand at acting in school productions, and began to teach the children's choir at her father's church in Rockville, where the family moved when she was 15. Wearing red leather pants, she shocked the mothers of the congregation, but their children adored her. Still, Myra Ellen began to get a little fed up with Jesus around this time.

"I used to get really pissed off that my life was so dictated by when this Jesus guy was born and when he was dying every year," she hissed in *Women, Sex And Rock'n'Roll*. **"I felt really**

resentful that I couldn't get on with my own life because I was so busy with his."

Myra Ellen had 75 kids to teach. Their mothers disapproved not only of her leather trousers, but also the way she referred to Jesus as *"that guy"*.

"They would say you called the Blood of Lamb 'that guy'? And I'd say I would call Jimmy Page 'that guy'."

Evidently Jimmy Page was up there with Jesus for Myra Ellen.

Saturday nights were reserved for making out with boyfriends in holly bushes, and when prayer meetings were held in the Amos family home, Myra Ellen would lie upstairs thinking forbidden thoughts.

"I'd think 'How do I escape this?'" she later confided to Liz Evans, "My song *Icicle* has a lot to do with it. It's about how this girl masturbates just to survive!"

She felt guilty about wanting to dissociate herself from her family's faith, she felt subjected to it, and suffered the usual internal struggles so familiar with teenagers who've been brought up in any blind, radical, or strict belief system. She was well aware that the church people were full of good intentions, but they had no truck with individuality, which is why she could never truly accept their fundamental beliefs, being very much an individual herself, and the battle to assimilate their ideas meant she had to cut out parts of herself.

"I had dead eyes," she recalled to Nick Coleman in the January 22-29, 1992 edition of Time Out, **"I let go of the things I believed in as a really young kid, and took on what they told me to believe in, and I don't just mean my parents. I had all my beliefs and feelings, all the things that were to do with me, crushed out of me."**

In autumn 1980, Myra Ellen made her very first record. Called Baltimore, the song had been co-written with her brother, Mike, and was a tribute to the local baseball team, the Baltimore Orioles. The song was released privately on her own label, MEA and won her a Citation from the Mayor.

On graduating from Montgomery High School, where she was voted *'Choir Flirt'* and Homecoming Queen, she persuaded her parents to let her study only music related subjects at Montgomery College, where she subsequently busied herself with drama, music and voice classes. She continued performing in the evenings at hotels and bars, covering everyone from The Doors to Barbra Streisand. The experience gave her a healthy background in the entertainment business at an early age, and although it would take her a while longer to retain her own personal control over her self expression, this grounding in the industry side was to prove invaluable.

Around this time, Myra Ellen became Tori. Her friend, Linda McBride, turned up with a date to watch her perform one night, and it was the date who provided the new name. He took one look at Myra Ellen, and declared that her name was in fact Tori, which actually means a type of pine tree. She liked it, it stuck, and Myra Ellen was consigned to the back benches.

Dr Amos continued to support his daughter in her burgeoning professional career by writing letters to unlikely characters such as Michael Jackson and Charlton Heston asking them for money for her. Needless to say, none of the stars provided sponsorship, and Tori carried on playing on local radio and television stations. Dr Amos posted off demo tapes to major labels, and eventually producer Narada Michael Walden expressed interest. Tori zoomed off to California to make a professional demo.

Her career suffered a slight setback the following summer when she was told by her doctor to remain silent for ten days. She had seriously hurt her vocal chords, and if she refused to listen to his instructions, she would do herself irreparable damage. Tori spent her time of confinement at her father's childhood home with her mother. It gave her the chance to sit back and contemplate things for a while, and she returned healed and refreshed.

The next stage of her life was about to begin. It would drain her and exhaust her, it would delight her and enable her to give vent to some of her more frustrated emotions, and it would nearly kill her. It would scar her for life, yet propel her further forward than she had ever been. It was all about to go off.

THE WRONG BAND

2

When Tori Amos was 21 she packed her bags, kissed goodbye to her choir and headed for the bright lights and the big city of Los Angeles. It was 1984, a time when all aspiring rock musicians were flinging their glad rags into the back of their beat up old Chevys and burning up into the sun. LA was the only option for anyone with a serious view to getting a record deal. Even New York paled in comparison for a while as the poodle rock bands with their big hair and sleazy songs took over the world. Sex filled the air, cartoon characters peopled the streets and raunch-driven riffs pumped out of clubs and bars. Glam and trash were the news, and Hollywood was high on it.

Tori felt like a kid in a candy shop. Everytime she left her house she was bombarded by beautiful sights. Men poured past her thick and fast, done up to the nines in their top rock garb. And she was free on Sundays!

"It was a very happy, perky time in LA." she told Liz Evans in *Women, Sex And Rock'n'Roll*, **"Everyone you met was in a band."**

"I'm glad that I sometimes pract

Living in East Hollywood, below Mann's Chinese Theatre near a whole bunch of musicians in the Beechwood district, Tori found the camaraderie she'd been searching for. Competition wasn't on the menu, just fun and games. Bands co-existed without bitterness, too caught up in the headiness of the scene to bother with bitching. After the strict musical environment Tori had witnessed at the Peabody, and the repressed religious atmosphere of her father's church, this was heaven.

She threw herself wholeheartedly into the party scene like a hungry lion, devouring whatever she could, stopping only to exercise enough caution to prevent her from getting sick. This was, after all, the boom of the AIDS era. Once she had the opportunity to sleep with two bisexual models, but declined.

"I'm glad that I sometimes, sometimes practiced caution." she said to Liz Evans, **"Sometimes. Enough."**

Tori took this time to explore a part of herself she had cut out to survive her upbringing. She neglected her music and expressed herself through her plastic snakeskin pants, bra tops and big hair. She joined a subculture, discovered the power of sexuality and closed down the part of herself which she no longer felt comfortable with. Fully aware of the DC Comics factor to the whole rock chick kudos, Tori revelled in the hardness lent to her by stiletto boots and studded leather. Putting two fingers up to the Reagan generation, together with her friends, she stomped about rebelliously with her tongue in her cheek.

"It's hard not to notice a girl with two-foot hair and plastic snakeskin boots up to her thighs, unfortunately." she confessed in good humour to VOX journalist Steve Malins. **"I was off to the races."**

On the musical front she was far from flagging, even though she was holding back from self expression. Within three weeks of arriving in LA, she had put a band together, but their first gig was a complete disaster, thanks to a varied mixture of drink, drugs and absence. Tori decided to return to piano bars to make a living. She gained further income from her brief stint making commercials (including one for Kellogg's Just Right cereal).

But around this time tragedy struck for Tori. One night an audience member offered her a ride home, and she was consequently raped at gunpoint by him. He threatened to kill her and furthermore, told her how he intended to do it. She survived by killing off the child in her, the part of her that would have given her game away by screaming and crying, the spirit in her which,

caution"

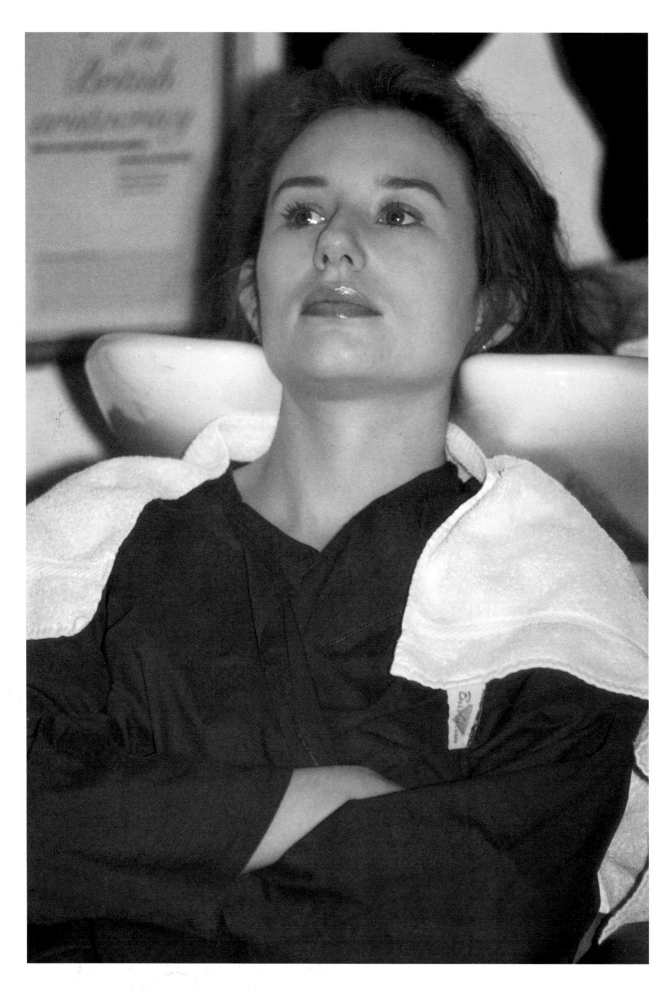

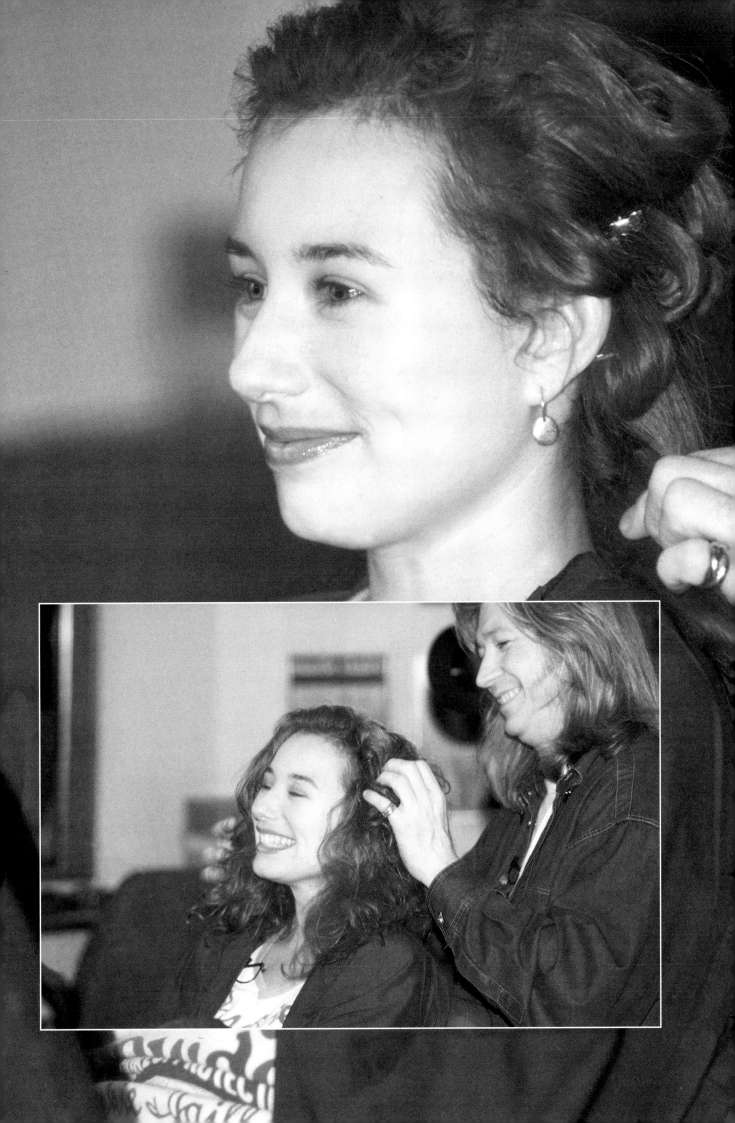

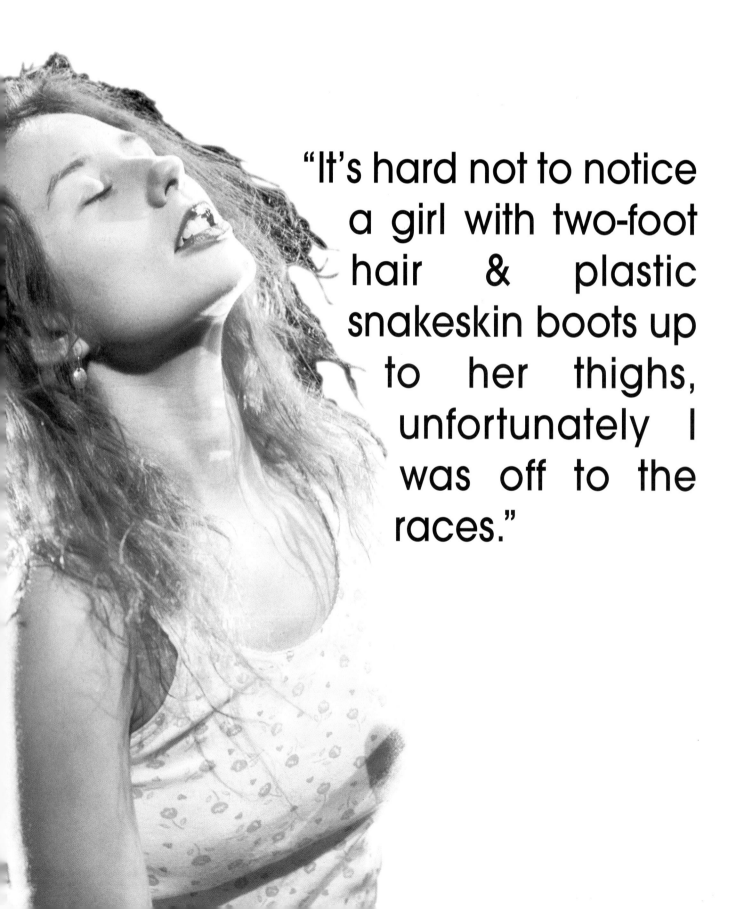

"It's hard not to notice a girl with two-foot hair & plastic snakeskin boots up to her thighs, unfortunately I was off to the races."

when confronted with a maniac, was a liability. She let the hooker take over.

"If the little girl had been operating I would be dead by now," Tori painfully related to Mark Edwards in *The Face.* **"I have no doubt of that because I was dealing with a maniac who wanted to cut women up. Put the sex aside for a while - this is about hatred. So my prostitute got me out of it - that side of me that understood what the energy this guy was feeding off was. Just keep him from going crazy. "**

The problem was, how to bring back the little girl? How to enjoy sex in a loving context again?

"For a long long time I had real difficulty having an intimate relationship with anyone," Tori told the Stud Brothers in the February 5th 1994 edition of *Melody Maker* ,"Every time I saw someone who looked like that guy I relived that night. Whenever I was being intimate with somebody it was like these veils came down. I couldn't see that men's strength and physicality could be tender. I had to pretend I was a whore in my mind, thinking I was gonna get paid so that I could be detached and stay in control."

Luckily, Tori met Eric Rosse. He forced her to take responsibility for having sex in a loving context, kept the lights on, and made her face up to what he was doing to her.

"He'll say 'What am I doing? I'm fucking you. Say it. And I love you. Say it.'"

Rosse and Tori were together for seven years. She has now left the relationship for a new and individual life, new adventures and different goals. But his commitment to help her heal herself has been unarguably invaluable to her.

At the time of her attack, Tori called her mother, who flew to LA to be with her daughter, and then she closed ranks on the incident and made herself a promise never to utter of it again. It was a promise she kept for six years.

Throwing herself into her work, Tori spent the next few years avoiding starvation and keeping a roof over her head. She put the girl and her piano to bed, blew her savings on recording equipment, and eventually, having assembled a band, she secured a deal with Atlantic Records and recorded the *Y Kant Tori Read* album.

By the time the album was released, the band had split up. Drummer Matt Sorum went on to play for Guns 'N' Roses, and the rest went their separate ways, although the guitarist would later hook up with Tori again for *Under The Pink.*

"I think the laug

r is what really got to me."

Y Kant Tori Read was a resounding flop. Even the magazines which bothered to review it had little to say other than that Tori was destined to failure. Billboard magazine, America's trade paper, had her down as a bimbo, and within three weeks of its release, her rock debut was no more than a bad memory. Tori took the rejection very badly. Having failed first her father, and now herself, she crumbled onto the kitchen floor and stayed there gazing at the lino.

The lowest point arrived when she was laughed out of Hugo's Restaurant, a frequent and favourite haunt of hers. Two tables of acquaintances (not friends she insists) from the music industry completely ignored her one night. A publisher and an A&R man, both of whom are probably kicking themselves now, began sniggering at her with their girlfriends, twisting the knife, while Tori stood there in her plastic thigh high boots and six inch high hair, eye smarting, relying on her 17 layers of waterproof mascara not to give the game away.

At that moment, she felt the four year old inside her reel. She had once been a child prodigy, and here she was, a laughing stock 20 years later.

"I think the laughter is what really got to me." Tori emphasised to Liz Evans, **"Because you have to remember where I came from. These people who were laughing at me were pissing on themselves when I could play concertos."**

Mortified, she tottered home and took refuge on the kitchen floor, collapsed like a pile of jelly. Finally she placed a call to Cindy Marble, a friend who sang with an unsigned band called The Rugburns. Cindy had an old piano, and asked Tori to go over and play for her. So she did. For five hours. And that was when she knew exactly what she had to do. There was no getting away from it. The piano was inextricably linked to her, and if she ever wanted to untie the knots which had been cluttering up her powers of real, true expression, she had to live with it.

The day after playing Cindy's piano, she rented one for her own apartment. Tori Amos - the real Tori Amos - was just about to be born.

"When you've been publicly humiliated, you're not even a cool cartoon character any more, you're a cartoon character that they're erasing .... and they have the power to erase you."

30

3
SILENT ALL THESE YEARS

Despite the miserable disaster of *Y Kant Tori Read?* Atlantic Records decided to take one more gamble on the singer who'd been laughed back to her kitchen. They gave her six months or so to come up with a new albums worth of material, but an insensitive visit from her label boss, who promptly called her new work ***"shit"*** (he was expecting Elton John from her) knocked her back into a depression again, and she didn't go near a piano for three months.

Although by now Tori had begun to slip out of the rock chick role, she started zipping herself back into it again after being insulted. Luckily her friends made her see sense, and guided her back to the keys. She underwent some un-traditional therapy, which involved talking to older, wiser people, and after some fairly incisive self examination, Tori started to tap into the well spring of repressed emotion which brought forth *Little Earthquakes*. For the first time since she was four, she started to write for the sole reason of expression. She wasn't doing it for her father, or to impress boys, or to get away from religion.

She was finally doing it for herself.

To wander right into herself, Tori created a symbolic environment at home. She laid out a faerie ring, and placed objects she felt some kind of affinity with inside it. She also put down some empty envelopes with the intention of giving each one of them a song title. Eventually she was ready to go by the end of March 1990, and together with some of the songs the label boss had previously dismissed, she submitted her work.

At first Atlantic weren't convinced by their artist. They sent Davitt Sigerson round to give her a helping hand, but fortunately for Tori, whose bleeding confidence couldn't sustain another bruise, he left without meddling, giving both Tori and Atlantic the necessary spark to see the album through. Tori entered the studio and soon had enough songs to fill a tape for the label. After a long and painful wait, Tori had her tape rejected, and this time she got angry.

Together with Eric Rosse, who was by now her partner, Tori recorded four songs at his home studio. Having dug so deep to get the first lot out, she had no intention of giving up, and this time it paid off. Atlantic decided to give Tori a go, but only on the condition that she wing it across to Britain where East West, their sister company would carefully introduce her to their more sympathetic and broad minded market. Apparently Americans might have taken to Tori had she been British herself, according to the reasoning minds at Atlantic. As if Tori cared.

When she reached London, Tori felt immediately at home. Her belief in past lives, her deep connections with the Celts and her love of history, her passion for the Norman invasion, her need to roam the countryside and visit ancient, mystical sites, as well as the old cities of romantic and classic literature filled her up with delight and intrigue. She revelled in it, and having acquainted herself so successfully with her new home, she set about playing low key gigs in small venues, such as The Borderline and The Mean Fiddler.

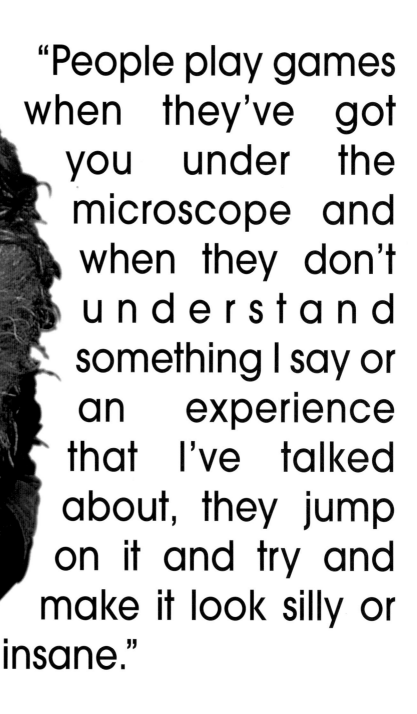

"People play games when they've got you under the microscope and when they don't u n d e r s t a n d something I say or an experience that I've talked about, they jump on it and try and make it look silly or insane."

As part of an ingenious marketing and press campaign, designed to let people think they had stumbled across a brilliant new secret, music journalists were treated to private showcases at the flat where Tori was staying. The word began to spread that there was a new genius in town, and before long Tori was giving interviews in her own inimitable style. For the uptight, cynical, unforgiving British music press, this presented a few problems.

As far as Tori was concerned she was just being honest. Telling it like it was. But the journalists she encountered had never met anyone quite like her, and always ready to have a go at someone, they immediately labelled her a *"kooky chick"*. One even went so far as to decry her *"mental decrepitude"*. Naturally this hurt Tori, who had taken years to find and formulate her own expression.

"People play games when they've got you under the microscope a nd when they don't understand something I say or an experience that I've talked about, they jump on it and try and make it look silly or insane."

Despite what the cynics said with their harsh and narrow-minded headlines, Tori was already making her mark. The first EP to be released, in October 1991, featured *Silent All These Years* and *Me And A Gun*, an acapella song which dealt with her feelings during her rape. She was inspired to write it after watching the rape scene in Thelma And Louise at the cinema,

and scribbled it out just before a North London gig. The press and promotion machines subtly kicked in, and before long Tori was performing on the Johnathan Ross Show and impressing the hell out of reviewers.

With top photographer and subsequent close friend, Cindy Palmano, Tori sculpted incredible visuals to accompany her work, developing a unique and striking image which said as much about her as her less than obvious songs. The pair worked by chatting with each other and floating ideas around in quite an abstract manner, with Cindy honing them into photographs and videos.

Another artist, Neil Gaiman, famous for his Sandman graphic novels also took inspiration from Tori, and injected it into one of his

characters, Delirium. Tori had already mentioned him by name in *Tear In Your Hand* and the pair struck up a friendship after she arranged for a tape of the song to be delivered personally to him. After meeting him, Tori insisted that she had known Neil in a past life.

Tori's debut album proper arrived in February 1992. Titled *Little Earthquakes*, it received geneous reviews, but didn't make an enormous dent on the listening public. Again, this was in keeping with East West's slow and deliberate build-up. Tori was shielded from press over exposure, getting just the right amount, and in the right places, to avoid the kind of saturation which so often damages new artists in Britain.

Tori's LA rock chick past was also

unearthed at this point, by the NME, and dealt her a vicious blow by intimating that her career change was due to a clever marketing plan and little else. Whoever pointed the finger was obviously missing the point by a million and one miles. Tori knew exactly what her past entailed, she'd enjoyed it and she wasn't ashamed of wearing snake-skin pants. She knew full well that she'd sold her soul by dumping the piano, which is precisely why she'd gone back to it for *Little Earthquakes*.

"Hey, I did that record." she declared emphatically to Liz Evans, **"I don't place blame. And hey, I chose to look like that too."**

Adverse publicity had little bearing on Tori's public appeal though, and when she started touring, her popularity rose dramatically. Her very intimate stage manner combined with her beautifully articulate and very personal songs to create a unique and special atmosphere. She travelled around Britain, America, Europe, and Australia, fitting in a holiday in Iceland and the MTV awards, where her parents were unflinchingly introduced to the likes of Pearl Jam and the Red Hot Chili Peppers. And then it was back to touring and promotion.

During her shows in America, especially down in the Bible belts, Tori managed to incur the wrath of feminists and religious mothers. Her style of playing the piano - twisted to face the audience, legs wide apart, pelvis grinding with the beat, head thrown back in ecstasy - has always been a sensual spectacle. But it is her expression, and she doesn't know how to play any other way. Evidently the uptight sisterhood and God-fearing crones couldn't cope.

> "These women were supposedly left-wing feminists, saying they were really offended by the way I was playing because I was making myself an object," a truly amazed Tori uttered to Liz Evans, "But I didn't see myself as an object. This was how I felt good playing. And I still do. It's a completely physical thing for me, the whole kundalini is very much involved. And you know what, the only place I've never felt guilty or shameful is when I've been playing."

Many more women responded to Tori's openness, her willingness to air her troubled past, and her warmth and optimism. She began to attract women who'd been abused or raped, and welcomed them all backstage with open arms and a boiling kettle. Eventually these intimate meetings with fans proved too much for her, but she kept them up until they were absolutely impossible to arrange.

In England an official fanzine called *Take To The Sky* appeared, and in America, *Really Deep Thoughts* provided a fan network. Finally, in November 1992, the Little Earthquakes tour reached its end. An exhausted, but overjoyed Tori made her way back to Britain's Q Magazine Awards where she received the *'Best New Act'* accolade, and where, perhaps more importantly, she finally got the chance to tell Robert Plant how she wanted to lose her virginity to him. He was suitably flattered, and the pair had their picture taken together, laughing and clutching each other like old friends. With *Little Earthquakes*, Tori Amos had shown the world her true and highly individual colours. Despite lame and easy comparisons to other female luminaries such as Patti Smith and Kate Bush (pulled out of the hat no doubt because of their gender and equally distinctive characters), Tori had proved herself to be an inimitable and highly original force. She had married her soul to a piano and laid it down before the world. And the world had walked straight into her heart, recognising something of their own irrationality, pain, turbulence, joy and delirium there. She had struck home. Her message had only just begun.

BELLS FOR HER

4

*L*ittle Earthquakes was Tori's acknowledgment of things which she'd kept beneath the stairs for 15 years. The rape she'd refused to deal with for five years, the claustrophobic religious atmosphere she'd been forced to adapt to as a child, the clipping of her creativity, her sometimes painful relationship with her father, and a myriad of other long hidden emotional and sexual areas sprang forth powerfully and beautifully, glad to see the light and breathe the air. But Tori still had a long way to go before all the various bits and pieces inside her were free. Having frozen up so many parts of herself in attempts to survive one situation after another, she could only warm up so many of them at a time, and with the next album, she was being led to deeper places. Little Earthquakes had been her diary. With her next album, she decided to *"put some clothes on."*

"That first album was very naked," Tori told the NME's Johnny Cigarettes in the 17 December 1994 edition. **"It was me rationalising my life at that point, like a diary. But to be honest**

I don't really wanna show the cellulite on my hip anymore. I've put some clothes on since then."

For Tori, the new album, *Under The Pink*, was more like an impressionist painting than an easily accessed journal. It had more layers, like a landscape, and she insisted her listeners should climb into the landscape to find out exactly what was going on there.

None of this was a deliberate choice on Tori's part. She views her songs as having their own autonomy. She claims not to be able to write under duress, but simply when the songs decide to come out. Some of them leap from her, others take ages. For her they already exist, she simply acts as a filter for them, similarly to Kristin Hersh of Throwing Muses, who speaks of her songs as having separate bodies and beings. Tori refers to her songs as her *"children"*, each with their own personality, and when the set for *Under The Pink* decided they wanted to put in an appearance, there wasn't very much she could do about it.

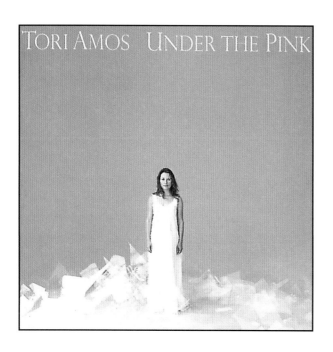

To record these songs, Tori chose to isolate herself in the desert of New Mexico. Together with her boyfriend Eric Rosse, who co-produced the album, and a whole fleet of equipment, she headed for a 150 year old hacienda in Taos, where she remained until the album was completed.

Staying in the desert was a very spiritual experience for Tori. She and Eric would drive out at night to watch the sunset by the Rio Grande with flasks of liquorice tea and blankets.

"This is sacred territory." she told Tim Rostron for the April 23, 1994 edition of The Daily Telegraph, **"Instead of bringing your vibe to a place, your vibe has to fit in. You're really out of order."**

With *Under The Pink* Tori wanted to get away from whatever victim status she had acquired, in the eyes of those who knew her for having been raped above all else. She wanted to get to show the survivor, the part of herself that could go out there with a box of matches and warm up all the frozen bits inside like a little pyro. She wanted to reach a place where she didn't have to feel crippled anymore, where she could be truly free and liberated, where she didn't have to suffer from feeling incomplete and disjointed inside. These new songs would help her begin to put a little more perspective on things, they would push her out of hiding a bit more.

With the help of Eric, who laboured over the technical side of things, exploring new

piano sounds and weird effects, Tori managed to produce a more complex and multi-textured album, just as she had hoped. Eric kept the red button on in the studio all the time, capturing *Bells For Her* unexpectedly, when it spilled out of Tori one day. He understood her habit of writing things on the spur of the moment, when she thought everyone else was out of earshot.

Another song, *Past The Mission* (for which Nine Inch Nails' Trent Reznor provided backing vocals) popped out as a direct result of being around all the missions, and what they represented for Tori in New Mexico, where there were so many, and hit single, *Cornflake Girl*, was inspired by Alice Walker's novel, *Possessing The Secret Of*

Joy, which dealt with female circumcision visited upon girls by their grandmothers. In fact, much of the album looked at female friendships and betrayals, why women let each other down, how much more painful it is to be betrayed by a woman friend than a boyfriend, and how this arises from female intimacy. Tori had been severely let down by a few of her own friendships, and wanted to confront the whole area.

"I've found more viciousness from women than from men, because men aren't really vicious. They can be ignorant and insensitive, and they sometimes lose control, but this sisterhood concept that I wanted to look at while I was growing up never materialised. And the older I've got the colder the water that's been poured on my head."

"I'm known as the girl who ha

Naturally male journalists questioned this gender traitor side, but she had answers for all of them - honest ones, which owed far more to the unpleasant truth of personal experience than sterile political correctness. Her problem with women who choose to deny their emotions, who behave towards each other competitively, made itself manifold, once more touching a sensitive and familiar nerve in her female listeners.

With *Under The Pink*, politically correct males and radical feminists were not the only factions of society to be upset by Tori's confrontational methods. While *Cornflake Girl* was the first single release in Britain, God was issued in America. Expressing Tori's long standing belief that God would be better off with a girlfriend, it was banned by mainstream radio, leaving the young college station listeners to appreciate her sentiment.

"I'm known as that girl who has tea with the Devil." she told Mark Edwards of *The Face.* **"I'm the thing that fundamentalist Christians cringe over. Mothers drag their daughters out of my shows. Because their daughters are going, 'Hey, maybe I don't have to think about these things. Why am I worshipping some dead guy?'"**

Interestingly Tori's father approved of the song.

Other songs, like *Baker Baker*, which addressed Tori's emotional unavailability after having suffered the rape, and *The Waitress*, which stood up to her violent side, (Tori calls her strong part Sven The Viking, and uses it to deal with difficult situations) continued her illuminating journey into the denied recesses of her spirit, while *Pretty Good Year* was a merciless response to a letter from an English boy fan who couldn't figure out what women wanted.

Although Tori was now dealing with different subjects through her songs, she was still being recognised for having brought the painful and traumatic experience of rape out into the open. And on June 2, 1994, she was awarded a Visionary Award by the Washington DC Rape Crisis Center for her work in dealing with the issues of rape and abuse. At the ceremony, Tori announced the opening of her Rape, Abuse and Incest National Network (RAINN), a free telephone support line for victims. As *Baker Baker* showed, although Tori no longer perceived herself to be a victim, she was still having difficulty opening up fully on a sexual and emotional level.

In a joint interview for *Q* magazine in 1994 with Polly Harvey and Björk, two equally unique and brilliant artists, Tori confessed that

ea with the devil"

sex for her was still a problematic area, despite Eric's support and understanding.

"I have a much harder time opening up in the intimate sex realm because I have stuff I have to deal with." she said. **"I don't have to go there emotionally when I play. I feel safe when I play. It's harder for me to feel that in sex."**

Evidently the attack of years earlier was still taking its toll. But Tori was about to push the boundaries of her life out, and change her emotional existence.

Another heavy touring schedule was undertaken by Tori to promote album number two, and during the latter half of 1994, she split with Eric, having decided that a change was necessary if she was to keep growing. This wrench was to affect her new material, the songs which would start to congregate after *Under The Pink* had been put to bed. As ever, the approach Tori's songs would take would depend upon convoluted emotion, contradiction, twists, turns, nuances, all the details which make blood pressures rise and hearts beat faster. Bearing her soul yet again, she was about to plunge into ever deeper waters.

5
PUTTING THE DAMAGE ON

As the millennium draws to a close, one woman's emotional and spiritual journey expands, taking in more weather, good and bad, covering more ground, rocky and smooth, unearthing terrain which hasn't seen sunlight for decades. Much has happened to her and experiences burst from her in songs plucked from another dimension. She tosses them back after soaking them in a private language which speaks loudly to the world. She gets braver all the time.

Tori Amos' new material has been greatly influenced by the ending of her seven year relationship with her partner and musical collaborator, Eric Rosse, the man who recorded one of her first demos for Atlantic Records in his home studio, and who co-produced *Under The Pink*. God knows how you leave a relationship like that, but as Tori divulged over a year ago, if you don't, you can't grow, you can't step forward on your journey. Nevertheless, breaking up is hard to do.

"How could we have been so cruel?" she implored of her failing partnership with Eric during an interview with Peter Paphides in the Christmas 1995 edition of *Time Out*.

"Because when we started there was so much love. Real caring. And I sit here hating this someone who I have been head over in heels with. Taking jets to meet up for four hours and then flying back to do a show the next night."

Tori and Eric split while she was in the middle of a 106 date sold out American tour. The new album, *Boys For Pele*, shows the strain. Full of songs which mourn the passing of love, which grapple to come to terms with an independent life after being so close for so long with someone, which try and face up to the ex having new loves, and which touch on the old themes of religion and female friendships, the record is deeply moving and very powerful.

Hey Jupiter , one of the record's most beautiful songs, confesses the pain and confusion of finally having to face up to the realisation of being completely without an ex-lover. Written after Tori placed numerous long distance and international calls to Eric's house in a moment of loneliness and weakness, it encapsulates the feeling of isolation which inevitably follows the breakdown of a long relationship, as she explained to Paphides.

"After all the...you know, the fiery red head behaviour, drawing my lines, making my

threats...I was lying there, feeling incredibly weak. Feeling like there are not enough sold-out shows, like it doesn't matter that every American show is sold out, because I'm only alive when I'm on stage with a piano. The rest of the time I'm just this shell."

Two years earlier, Tori had said more or less the same thing to Liz Evans, in her book, *Women, Sex And Rock'n'Roll.*

"Playing is the only place where I've felt in touch with my sexuality, my spirituality and my emotions, and never, ever, ever anywhere else. So my life is a bit tricky because when I'm not playing, I'm just trying to walk down the street."

With *Boys For Pele*, the conflicts rage on. *Putting The Damage On* speaks of the lingering attraction for the ex love, and the brave face required to see it through, as if a mask is necessary to let someone go - for both parties. The

new single, *Caught A Lite Sneeze* is a cry for help from a lone woman in a time of crisis, looking for female support in a male dominated world. *Blood Roses* looks at the cutting out of parts of the self to survive and forget, and seems to be dealing with the way Tori coped with the aftermath of being raped, by divorcing her spirit from her body during sex. *Muhammed My Friend* questions the patriarchal sensibilities of organised world religions, echoing one of Tori's favourite Goddess themes, Talula returns to the subject of lost love,

this time with the added convolution of new love (in the case of the ex) and a new life, *Doughnut Song* continues the theme, but with different textures, *In The Springtime Of His Voodoo* (the title of which carries echoes of Led Zeppelin) deals with sex and religion, and finally, *Twinkle* brims with hope and strength, taking its inspiration from a star.

Of course Tori's songs, being so full of layers, are wide, wide open to interpretation. Her meanings have a life of their own, and are rarely instantly recognisable. So treat the above as a rough guide, a personal interpretation - not gospel.

Other songs on the new album are equally opaque on first listening, requiring time and attention to fully appreciate. Riddled with personal references (like the Fig Newtons in Talula - which were biscuits Tori and Eric would eat by the sunset at Rio Grande after dinner in the desert, during the making of *Under The Pink*), and names of friends (naturally Neil Gaiman crops up again, in *Horses*), they remain very much her own property, but in dealing with the universal questions of love, sex and religion, speak to her listening public as well.

Tori Amos has done it again. Delved deep into her heart, pulled out the darkest and the brightest things in there, and laid them out in complex patterns and abstract forms. She connects on the most fundamental level, where language breaks up and emotions and music take over. She spins with her spirit, and there is no stronger thread than that.